Michelle   Man

A CHRISTMAS CAROL

CHARLES DICKENS

www.realreads.co.uk

Retold by Gill Tavner
Illustrated by Karen Donnelly

Published by Real Reads Ltd
Stroud, Gloucestershire, UK
www.realreads.co.uk

First published in 2007
Reprinted 2010, 2011, 2012 (twice), 2013

ISBN 978-1-906230-02-9

Printed in China by Wai Man Book Binding (China) Ltd
Designed by Lucy Guenot
Typeset by Bookcraft Ltd, Stroud, Gloucestershire

CONTENTS

THE CHARACTERS

Scrooge

A mean, miserable, lonely old miser. Can he learn the truth about Christmas and about himself before it is too late?

Bob Cratchitt

Scrooge's poor office clerk and a loving father. Can he earn enough money to save his son's life?

Tiny Tim

Bob's gentle, frail son. Will he live or will he die?

Jacob Marley's ghost

Scrooge's dead business partner.
Will his terrible warning
come too late?

Ghost of Christmas Past

Why does this ghost make Scrooge
weep with both joy and sorrow?

Ghost of Christmas Present

A cheerful spirit. Will Scrooge
heed his warnings?

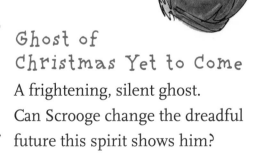

Ghost of Christmas Yet to Come

A frightening, silent ghost.
Can Scrooge change the dreadful
future this spirit shows him?

A CHRISTMAS CAROL

'Bah, humbug,' complained Scrooge. 'Fools wishing me a Merry Christmas should be forced to sit on cushions stuffed with holly leaves or boiled with their own Christmas puddings. Go away and take your "Merry Christmas" with you.'

'But Uncle, I'm wishing you a merry Christmas in spite of yourself. Remember,' shouted Scrooge's beaming, rosy-cheeked nephew, turning back as he left the office, 'you are welcome to join us for Christmas dinner.' As the nephew left, his warmth went with him. Now the office was cold. Cold is cheap, and Scrooge liked it that way.

In the dim light of his inadequate fire, Scrooge muttered 'Humbug' again, and went back to counting his money.

At another desk in the same room, Scrooge's office clerk, Bob Cratchitt,

sat scribbling furiously. He had wished
Scrooge's nephew a Merry Christmas, and felt
afraid of Scrooge's reaction.

'And you, Bob Cratchitt, what right has
someone as poor as you to be merry?'

'I'm sorry, Mr Scrooge.'

'I suppose you would like to stay at home tomorrow to spend Christmas with your children?'

'I would dearly love it, sir.'

'Why should I pay you for a day at home? Christmas is just an excuse for picking my pocket. I shall expect you in early the next day to make up for it.'

'Yes, certainly, Mr Scrooge.'

Poor Bob pulled his scarf more tightly around his neck and blew on his hands in a vain attempt to warm them. He returned to his work. The one coal that Scrooge allowed on the fire was dying, and with it the slight warmth that it brought.

But for Scrooge's clinking money and Bob's scratching pen the room was silent.

Clang! The bell above the door clanged its cheerless clang, announcing the arrival of another unwelcome visitor.

'Merry Christmas, sir,' said a portly smiling gentleman.

'Is it?' muttered Scrooge.

'It certainly should be, sir. Christmas is a time for goodness, for generous giving. I am collecting for homeless children, that they might be sheltered and fed this Christmas.'

'What!' exclaimed Scrooge, 'Are there no prisons, no workhouses to do this job?'

'Unfortunately, sir, there are plenty of both.'

'Then the beggars have no need of my charity,' grumbled Scrooge. His cold hands ushered the stunned gentleman back out through the door, the bell clanging farewell.

Bob coughed and rubbed his hands together. His employer was a grasping, scraping, selfish, cold old sinner, hard and sharp, and very lonely.

As Bob reached for a new coal for the fire, Scrooge snapped at him. 'Go on then. Go and join the other fools out there.'

'Thank you, sir,' Bob scuttled to the door, hurriedly putting on his coat before

Scrooge could change his mind. 'And a Merry Christm—'

'Go!' shouted Scrooge. 'Humbug,' he muttered as the clanging bell echoed his loneliness.

The fire dead, the candle extinguished, and the cashbox firmly locked, Scrooge pulled the door closed behind him as he stepped out into the street. He looked up at the sign above the shop door – 'Scrooge and Marley' it said, even though Jacob Marley had been dead seven years. Scrooge hadn't bothered to paint out the 'Marley' – it would cost money for someone to do it. Sometimes people new to the business called Scrooge 'Scrooge', and sometimes 'Marley', but he answered to both names. It was all the same to him. What was not in doubt, however, was that Marley was dead, utterly dead, dead as a doornail. Scrooge, the sole mourner at his funeral, had seen his coffin lowered into the ground.

The cold and dampness felt comfortable to Scrooge, unlike the cheerful faces of the hurrying people around him, people eager to be home with their families, people eager to prepare their Christmas dinners. Although most of them avoided Scrooge, he felt attacked by their happiness, offended by their smiles, and he hid in a shop doorway to avoid the horror of a young boy singing Christmas carols.

'Bah. Humbug.'

Eventually he reached his front door, having taken a longer route than usual to avoid yet more carol singers. Scrooge slid the key into the lock. As he did so, something made him jump back. He gasped. He stared. The old brass knocker on his door appeared to have developed a face. Scrooge blinked to make the image disappear. It stayed. The face's deadly cold eyes

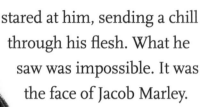

stared at him, sending a chill through his flesh. What he saw was impossible. It was the face of Jacob Marley.

Hesitantly, Scrooge entered his cold, dark house. The door slammed behind him.

'Nonsense,' he attempted to convince himself. 'Stuff and nonsense.' It was dark inside the house, but Scrooge decided not to light a candle. Darkness was cheap, and Scrooge liked it that way. He glanced back at his front door, then felt his way up the stairs. Once in his room, he looked carefully around before undressing, climbing into bed, and pulling the covers tightly over his head.

Cold, dark and still. No sound but his own breathing. Scrooge was disturbed by the vision of Jacob Marley in his front door knocker, and was finding it difficult to sleep.

Jingle. Scrooge stirred. *Tinkle.* Scrooge's wide eyes peeped above his covers. *Jangle.* Scrooge's eyes were drawn towards the movement of a bell, old, dusty and unused these many years, which hung in the corner of his room. It was now swinging vigorously. *Clatter. Clang. Bang. CLANG. BANG! CRASH!*

This wasn't just the bell. There were loud noises outside his bedroom door. A booming sound echoed up his staircase.

BANG!!!

The door was blasted open by a violently cold wind. Scrooge shot bolt upright in his bed. Through the darkness he once again saw the deadly cold eyes of Jacob Marley. As Scrooge stared, he noticed that Marley, or rather, Marley's ghost, was bound by heavy iron with

chains, padlocks and cash boxes that clanged
when he moved.

'Nonsense,' muttered Scrooge, trying to
settle himself again. 'Just a bad dream. I must
have eaten too much cheese.'

'No, Ssscrooge, this isn't a dream,'
whispered the spirit, 'Nor is it a nightmare.

Ssscrooge, thisss isss real.' It gave a frightful cry, echoed by a frightened yelp from Scrooge. Marley clattered his chains.

'Sssee, sssee these chainsss. Sssee these chainsss,' whispered Marley.

'I—I see them.'

'Hear, hear my wordsss. Hear my wordsss.'

'I—I hear them.'

'Thessse chainsss I made during my earthly life. For thessse passst ssseven yearsss I have been sssleeplesss, ressstlesss, knowing only remorssse and sssorrow,' he continued in a whisper like a sad, lonely breeze. 'I ssspent many ssselfish yearsss doing businesss, ignoring, as you do, the more important businesss of mankind. Now I pay. Now I pay and I sssuffer.'

'Humbug. Nonsense. Bad dream,' said Scrooge firmly, blinking hard.

'Lisssten,' continued the spirit, 'whilssst you have the chance. Sssee through your window.'

Obeying, Scrooge was chilled to the core as he saw the cold night sky fill with spirits, all chained like Marley.

'We all made othersss sssuffer. Now the sssuffering isss our own. We are eternally doomed to wander thisss earth, ssseeking to do good but forever missserable that we have lossst the power to do ssso.'

Scrooge stared in horror.

'You ssstill have a chance of essscaping thisss fate,' whispered the ghost, now chillingly close. Expect three more ssspirits.'

'No, please,' begged Scrooge.

'Expect them,' the spirit faded into the night sky, 'expect them.'

Exhausted, Scrooge stumbled backwards against his bed.

'Humbug,' he muttered as he slid into a restless sleep.

Scrooge was awakened by his clock striking one. He held his breath and peeped out of the safety of his covers. Nothing. He breathed a sigh of relief.

Like a bolt of lightning, a bright flash filled the room as the curtains around his bed were flung violently apart. Scrooge gasped. His heart thumped as his eyes struggled to adjust to the light. The figure gradually becoming clear to him was small and fresh-faced like a young boy, but long grey hair and sinuous arms made him look grotesquely old. The strangest thing was that from the top of his head sprang a bright, clear fountain of light.

'What, or who, are you?' ventured Scrooge.

'I am the Ghost of Christmas Past.'

'Long past?'

'No. Your past. Don't be afraid, I have come to do you good.'

'I can't help thinking that a good night's sleep would have done me more good,'

observed Scrooge, trying to break the solemn atmosphere. The spirit ignored him.

'Come with me,' it beckoned, walking towards the window. 'Touch my heart and you will fly with me.'

Scrooge did as he was instructed, and found himself flying through the night sky. They flew away from London's mist to beautiful fields filled with snow, and so many happy children that it seemed the crisp, cold air itself was laughing.

'Why do you weep?' asked the spirit, observing Scrooge closely.

'I was a boy here,' whispered Scrooge, 'I was a boy.'

They came to rest in a cold classroom, empty but for one boy sitting in a corner reading.

'That's me,' sobbed Scrooge, 'poor, lonely Ebenezer Scrooge. I spent many Christmases here with only my books for company.'

'Until ...' said the spirit, inviting Scrooge to continue.

'Until the time my sister Fan took me home,' remembered Scrooge softly. As he watched, the young Scrooge in the classroom grew a few years older. The boy paced around the room, waiting for something, or someone. With a blast of energy, the door burst open and a lively girl, all smiles and hugs, ran straight to him. 'Father has grown kinder,' she laughed. 'You are to come home forever.'

'Dear, dear sister' said the boy, holding her tightly and laughing with joy.

'My dear, dear sister,' repeated the old miser Scrooge, as tears fell freely down his cheeks. 'She grew to be a wonderfully kind woman,' he said to the spirit.

'I know,' came the gentle reply. 'She died, did she not, some years ago, leaving just one son?'

'My nephew,' sighed Scrooge, wishing at that moment that he could talk to his nephew.

'Come, come, time is short.' The spirit clicked his fingers, hurrying Scrooge on.

The scene now changed before Scrooge's eyes. He found himself tapping his feet and smiling, unable to resist some merry melodies being played on a frisky fiddle. Around him, forty laughing people danced and clapped.

They danced in and out, pranced up and down, bumped into one another; they apologised before moving on and standing on another person's toes. Bright-eyed, red-cheeked and out of breath, they rested, drank, and danced once again as the irresistible fiddle struck up a fresh tune.

On the tables was a magnificent spread of turkey, ham, mince pies, Christmas cake and plenty of beer, to which the dancers joyfully helped themselves.

'Scrooge, my boy,' smiled a fat, jovial voice, 'Merry Christmas!'

The older Scrooge watched a younger version of himself raising his glass and calling back 'Merry Christmas, Mr Fezziwig!'

'Why, it's old Fezziwig!' gasped Scrooge, 'He was my employer.'

'Was he a good man to work for?' asked the spirit.

'Oh, the best!' exclaimed Scrooge enthusiastically. 'He had the power to make

us happy or unhappy, to make our work a
pleasure or a toil – and he always chose to
make us happy.'

'How wonderful to work for such a
generous man,' observed the spirit, watching
Scrooge carefully.

'Yes, indeed,' sighed Scrooge, wishing
at that moment that he could talk to Bob
Cratchitt.

The spirit clicked his fingers again, and a
new scene flickered into view. A pretty
young lady was weeping, handing a ring
to the solemn-faced young man sitting next
to her.

'You are no longer the boy I loved,' she
sobbed. 'You think only of gain and of gold.
You have become grasping and cold.'

'But wealth is important for our future,'
argued the young man.

'Love and goodness are more important, and they are dying within you. I can no longer marry you.'

Distressed, the jilted young Scrooge took back his ring and slipped it into his pocket.

The older Scrooge fell to his knees. 'Oh please, please let this torment end,' he begged of the spirit.

The spirit turned away and put on his hat. Immediately the light issuing from the crown of his head was extinguished. Scrooge was alone in his cold, dark bedroom. He sobbed himself to sleep.

Scrooge woke himself with a particularly loud snore. Alarmed, he glanced at his clock. His alarm turned to amazement when, for the second time that night, the clock struck one o'clock.

Warily, Scrooge poked one bare foot from his bed. He stood up and tiptoed, trembling, to the door. Opening it slightly, he put his eye to the tiny crack. Another eye stared back at him. Scrooge leapt back, and the door burst open.

A jolly giant of a man strode into the room. Carrying a glowing torch, he cast light into every corner of the room. His magnificent green robe was bordered with fur. His long, dark curly hair framed his friendly face. His eyes sparkled.

'I am the Ghost of Christmas Present,' his glorious voice rang out.

'Please teach me your lessons. I feel that I am learning well.' Scrooge's voice was a mouse's squeak in contrast.

'Follow me,' laughed the spirit, his strong arm around Scrooge's shoulders. They went outside, where the damp morning mist and the dirty melting snow framed the gloomy London scene Scrooge knew so well. Yet at the same time there was an air of cheerfulness around,

and the people who were shovelling the
snow away were jovial and full of glee.
Snowballs whizzed and splattered on laughing
faces. Bustling between brightly-lit, glowing
shops, the glowing people ran and dashed,
forgetting their quarrels and full of the spirit
of human love.

Inside the shops, oh what a sight! Onions sat in their baskets like jolly old men, French plums blushed modestly as shelves of rosy apples flirted with customers. Turkey and goose hung deliciously from rails, awaiting the chance to grace a family's Christmas table.

Baskets clattered, cash tills chinged cheerfully. People forgot their purchases and came dashing back, laughing at their mistake.

The church bells rang their invitation and the crowds flocked towards them, heading to the centre of their Christmas joy. It was Christmas Day, and the Ghost of Christmas Present watched it all with pleasure. So did Scrooge.

The spirit guided Scrooge a few streets further on, where they saw Bob Cratchitt striding towards a front door, carrying a small boy on his shoulders. They followed him into the warmth of the Cratchitt kitchen.

Scrooge felt that his nose was not big enough to breathe in all the wonderful smells. The goose, although barely big enough to feed the family, sat crisp and proud, awaiting carving; the vegetables bubbled excitedly and the pudding steamed and steamed, creating a sweetly scented heaven in which the family revelled.

Bob's happy wife, her worn-out clothes decorated with cheerily cheap ribbons, was making the brandy butter, whilst their eldest daughter stirred the gravy and their eldest son checked the water for the potatoes. Two young Cratchitts ran excitedly around the kitchen.

In the other room, now down from Bob's
shoulders, Tiny Tim helped his father prepare
the table.

Tiny Tim was a pale, frail little boy with
the face of an angel. Scrooge noticed that he
walked with the aid of a crutch, and that his
weak legs were supported by iron frames.

He offered his father what little help he could before sitting wearily in his chair.

The children ran in ahead of Mrs Cratchitt, who was nervously carrying the goose. As Bob carved, everybody expressed amazement at the tenderness of the meat. Nobody commented on how small it was for such a large family.

'We are all so fortunate to have each other,' mused Tiny Tim. 'I hope that we can remember children less fortunate than us in our prayers.' He looked down at his thin, weakening legs. 'I hope too,' he said to Bob, 'that I can be stronger in spirit than I am in body, and so do some good in this world for as long as I am able to stay in it.'

As dinner was served, Tiny Tim, in his fragile voice, sang a prayer of thanks. Fighting back a tear, Bob held Tim's withered little hand in his own.

'A Merry Christmas to us all, my dears. God bless us,' beamed Bob.

'Merry Christmas,' chorused the family.

'God bless us every one,' concluded Tim.

Scrooge looked at Tim. 'Tell me Spirit, will Tiny Tim live?' he asked the spirit anxiously.

'I see a vacant seat at next year's table. If these shadows remain unaltered by the future, the child will die,' answered the spirit sadly.

'Oh no. Say that he will be spared.'

'Only if the family's fortunes change.'

Scrooge thought carefully about this. Who had the power to change this family's future? Who could save this precious child and spare the family's heartbreak?

The spirit spoke sternly. 'You have sometimes said that a poor person's death is one less mouth to feed, have you not?'

Scrooge lowered his head in shame.

'It may be that, in the sight of heaven, you yourself are less fit to live than millions like this poor man's child.'

'I am sure of it,' whispered Scrooge.

The spirit gently pointed back to the dinner table, where the joyful atmosphere had suddenly faded.

'Why should we drink a toast to that mean, hard, unfeeling Scrooge, father?'

'Because it is Christmas, and because he is alone,' explained Bob.

'It is very difficult to do when he has been so mean to you and made life so hard for us,' said Tiny Tim.

Bob squeezed Tim's hand. 'At Christmas, of all times, we should forgive.'

They raised their glasses. 'To Mr Scrooge,' they said solemnly. Duty over, their happiness returned and the house was once again filled with laughter.

Stepping back into the bustling streets, Scrooge noticed that the spirit had grown strangely older. His hands grasped the thin wrists of two small children, withered by hunger. The children glared menacingly at Scrooge.

'Who—who are these children?'

'They are the children we have created. Angels should live within these tiny bodies, but devils now occupy the space. Poverty has taught them misery and anger. Our society has made them what they are, and our society should beware of the monsters they will become.'

As they arrived back at Scrooge's house the spirit disappeared, but the children faded more slowly. Thoughts of poverty, of angels, of devils, and of Tiny Tim swirled in Scrooge's head, spinning him dizzily to sleep.

The next time Scrooge was awoken, it was by his clock striking twelve times. He suspected this was the prelude to the appearance of another ghost. Opening his eyes, he saw a draped and hooded spirit floating like a mist towards him.

'Are you the Spirit of Christmas Yet to Come?'

Covered entirely in black, with only one skeletal arm exposed, the spirit filled Scrooge with horror and dread. Although he was by now used to ghostly company, Scrooge feared the silent shape so much that his legs trembled under him, and he found that he could hardly stand when he prepared to follow it.

'Show me what you will. Dreadful though you are, I believe that you will help me.'

The bare white arm pointed to the door. Scrooge obeyed, and immediately found himself in Bob Cratchitt's living room.

'Father trudges home so slowly these days,' observed the eldest son.

'He used to trot to and fro when he carried Tiny Tim on his shoulders,' agreed Mrs Cratchitt. 'I suppose Tim was very light to carry, and your father loved him so much.'

The family fell silent. Waiting. Each one lost in their own sorrow. Tiny Tim's little crutch rested against the wall beside the fire. Mrs Cratchitt wiped a disobedient tear from her cheek. Scrooge did the same.

'Father!' shouted one of the younger children, rushing to embrace Bob as he walked through the door. 'Where have you been?'

'I promised that I would visit his grave every Sunday,' replied Bob, struggling to sound cheerful. Catching sight of the crutch, he broke down. 'My little child. My dear little child.'

Bob's children, full of life and love, ran to him. One took his scarf, one brought him a warm drink, and the other two led him to his chair. Climbing onto his knees, they wrapped

their arms around their father and covered his
face with tender kisses.

'We will never forget Tiny Tim,' comforted
Mrs Cratchitt.

'We must never forget his mildness of

spirit,' added Bob, composing himself. 'His generous, gentle nature should guide us all.'

'Oh, it will, father, it will.'

'Oh, my Tiny Tim.'

'Please, please take me away from this,' begged Scrooge, tears streaming down his cheeks. The spirit turned and pointed to a street which Scrooge recognised as the city's business district. Two smartly dressed gentlemen were talking as they strode along.

'I know them!' boasted Scrooge. 'I often do business with them. They hold me in high regard, and I have great respect for their opinions.'

The spirit signalled that Scrooge should stop talking and listen.

'Well, well,' said the taller man, 'few will mourn his death. Indeed, I'm sure many will celebrate the end of their debts.'

'I passed by his office this afternoon,' reported the shorter man. 'His servants were sharing out his goods between themselves. They had taken the curtains and blankets from his bed.'

'Oh, how terrible.'

'That's not all. They had removed the clothes from his dead body as it lay there, unwatched, unwept and uncared for.'

The taller man gasped in horror. 'So his body lies there still?'

'Yes. He died alone and remains alone in death, except for the rats. Had he been a pleasant man, somebody would have been there to care for him.'

'Very true. Well, the world is a happier place without him.'

'Who is this poor man of whom they talk?' asked Scrooge, fearing the answer. The spirit led him to the churchyard and pointed to a newly engraved headstone. Scrooge saw the name

EBENEZER SCROOGE

Scrooge trembled. His legs, giving up their struggle to support him, threw him to the ground. 'Please say that these things can be changed. Please. I will honour Christmas with all my heart, and try to keep its spirit every day of the year. Please say that this can change.'

Scrooge awoke the next morning with considerable
relief. He was alive! His blankets and curtains
were still there! He was still in his pyjamas! He
experienced the unusual sensation of his heart
leaping for joy within his breast.

'I don't know what to do!' he shouted,
laughing and crying. For someone so out of
practice, his laugh was magnificent. He attempted
to spring out of bed. This needed more practice.

Picking himself off the floor, Scrooge darted around his room. 'I am as light as a feather, as wobbly as a jelly, as silly as a sausage, as happy as a lark!'

Outside, the bells merrily jingled their Christmas morning melody.

'It's Christmas Day! Hooray!'

Scrooge dressed quickly and pattered downstairs, forgetting his shoes. The day was crisp and bright. 'Merry Christmas!' he shouted to his astounded neighbours. 'What a wonderful knocker!' he exclaimed, giving the knocker on his door a grateful polish.

'Here, boy!'

A young boy timidly obeyed Scrooge's call.

'Take this money. Go and buy the biggest turkey you can find and take it immediately to Bob Cratchitt's house. Oh, and keep the change.'

Still in his socks, Scrooge walked amongst the people in the street. 'Merry Christmas!' he called, 'God bless you all.'

He decided that he would accept his nephew's invitation to Christmas dinner this year. That would surprise them! First, however, he must visit a very special family.

Gathered around an enormous turkey, Bob and his family looked bemused. When Scrooge looked through the window, Tiny Tim was nowhere to be seen. When an anxiously-smiling Scrooge stepped through the door, a small yelp of fear came from behind the turkey. Scrooge peered over the enormous bird, and there was Tiny Tim.

'Tim, my precious boy! You are still here!' With tears streaming down his cheeks, and his arms outstretched as if to welcome an embrace, Scrooge stepped towards Tiny Tim. Tim stepped back in terror. Poor Bob, trembling, ushered his family into the safety of the living room. He thought of grabbing the carving knife and calling for help. Surely Scrooge had gone mad!

'Bob Cratchitt, I wish to raise your salary,' grinned Scrooge. It took him several long minutes to calm Bob's fears, and several more to convince him that he really wished to help.

An hour later, happily dozing by Bob's fire with Tiny Tim nestled snugly on his knee, Scrooge suddenly started. His nephew had invited him, Scrooge, to join his family for Christmas dinner, and he had nearly forgotten!

Swiftly kissing every Cratchitt on the cheek, he pranced lightly out of the door in his stockinged feet. As he left, he called back into the house, 'Merry Christmas! God bless you all!'

'God bless us every one,' replied Tiny Tim.

TAKING THINGS FURTHER

The real read

This *Real Read* version of *A Christmas Carol* is a retelling of Charles Dickens' magnificent work. If you would like to read the full novel in all its original splendour, many complete editions are available, from bargain paperbacks to beautifully bound hardbacks. You may well find a copy in your local charity shop.

Filling in the spaces

The loss of so many of Charles Dickens' original words is a sad but necessary part of the shortening process. We have had to make some difficult decisions, omitting subplots and details, some important, some less so, but all interesting. We have also, at times, taken the liberty of combining two events into one, or of giving a character words or actions that originally belong to another. The points below will fill in some of the gaps, but nothing can beat the original.

- After seeing Marley's face in the doorknocker, Scrooge sees it again in a carving on his mantelpiece.

- When the Ghost of Christmas Past takes Scrooge to visit his school, there is another classroom scene. We see a young Scrooge all alone at Christmas, reading books. His loneliness is evident when he treats the characters in his books as his friends.

- The Ghost of Christmas Present takes Scrooge to see his former fiancée, Belle, and her husband. Her husband says that he saw Scrooge in the street that day, and tells Belle that Scrooge is a lonely man.

- The Ghost of Christmas Present takes Scrooge to see his nephew Fred's party. The scene is one of great enjoyment: fun, games, flirtation and an engagement. Scrooge enjoys the party, but cannot be seen by the others.

- The businessmen who refer to Scrooge's death did not witness his servants sharing his possessions.

- Scrooge is shown poor people, in a poor alleyway, comparing the goods they stole from his house and attempting to sell them.

- Scrooge sees some people who owed someone money expressing relief at his death.

- On Christmas Day, Scrooge apologises to the man who asked for charity at the beginning of the novel. He sends a turkey to Bob's house and attends his nephew's party.

- The following day, in his office, he promises Bob a pay rise and says that he will help his family.

- At some time in the future we see Scrooge enjoying spending time with Bob's family.

Back in time

The population of Victorian London was increasing rapidly, partly due to immigrants from Ireland who were escaping the potato famine, and partly from migration from the countryside caused by the industrial revolution. This made it very difficult to find work. People like Bob Cratchitt were therefore paid very low wages – barely enough to live on.

Many in London were living in great poverty. Whilst the wealthy made more and more money, the poor died of disease and starvation. Many people who were reasonably well off, like Scrooge, felt that poverty was a sign of weakness or laziness. The Poor Laws of 1834 stated that people could only receive assistance from the state if they lived and worked in workhouses. Debtors were put in prison. Remember Scrooge's comment to the man collecting for charity?

Charles Dickens experienced poverty at first hand – his father was imprisoned for debt and the young Charles made to work in a warehouse. These experiences affected him deeply.

Unlike Scrooge, some Victorians were concerned by this poverty and devoted themselves to helping others. Dr Barnardo set up his first school in 1870, twenty-seven years after the first publication of *A Christmas Carol*.

Ghost stories became very popular in Victorian times. New capabilities of the human mind were being explored and discovered. Many of these advances must have amazed people. They probably felt that if there was a lot about the natural world that was beyond their knowledge or understanding, the same could be true of the supernatural world.

Charles Dickens played a central role in exploring the idea of the supernatural in Victorian literature. Whilst it greatly interested him, he urged critical investigation rather than unthinking belief.

Finding out more

We recommend the following books and websites to gain a greater understanding of Charles Dickens' and Scrooge's London:

Books

- Terry Deary, *Loathsome London* (Horrible Histories), Scholastic, 2005.

- Terry Deary, *Vile Victorians* (Horrible Histories), Scholastic, 1994.

- *Victorian London*, Watling Street Publishing, 2005.

- Ann Kramer, *Victorians* (Eyewitness Guides), Dorling Kindersley, 1998.

- Peter Ackroyd, *Dickens*, BBC, 2003.

Websites

- www.victorianweb.org
Scholarly information on all aspects of Victorian life, including literature, history and culture.

- www.bbc.co.uk/history/british/victorians
The BBC's interactive site about Victorian
Britain, with a wide range of information and
activities for all ages.

- www.dickensmuseum.com
Home of the Dickens Museum in London,
with details about exhibits, events and lots of
helpful links.

- www.dickensworld.co.uk
Dickens World, based in Chatham in Kent, is
a themed visitor complex featuring the life,
books and times of Charles Dickens.

- www.charlesdickenspage.com
A labour of love dedicated to Dickens, with
information about his life and his novels.
Many useful links.

- www.barnardos.org.uk/who_we_are/
history.htm
An interesting description of the conditions in
Victorian London that inspired Dr Barnardo to
devote his life to helping poor children.

Food for thought

Here are some things to think about if you are reading *A Christmas Carol* alone, or ideas for discussion if you are reading it with friends.

In retelling *A Christmas Carol* we have tried to recreate, as accurately as possible, Dickens' original plot and characters. We have also tried to imitate aspects of his style. Remember, however, that this is not the original work; thinking about the points below, therefore, can help you begin to understand Charles Dickens' craft. To move forward from here, turn to the full-length version of *A Christmas Carol* and lose yourself in his wonderful storytelling.

Starting points

- How do you feel about Scrooge at the beginning of the book?

- What clues are there that Scrooge has not always been a miser?

- Which ghost do you find the most frightening? Why?

- Which experiences do you think affect Scrooge the most? Why do you think this?

- What do you think Scrooge has learned by the end of the story?

- Which description of Christmas do you like best?

Themes

What do you think Charles Dickens is saying about the following themes in A Christmas Carol?

- Christmas
- poverty
- society
- family life
- charity

Style

Can you find paragraphs containing examples of the following?

- descriptions of setting and atmosphere

- the use of simile, onomatopoeia and personification to enhance description

- emotive writing

- humour

- the use of a very simple sentence to achieve a particular effect

Look closely at how these paragraphs are written. What do you notice? Can you write a paragraph in the same style?